Superphonics® **Storybooks** will help your child to learn to read using Ruth Miskin's highly effective phonic method. Each story is fun to read and has been carefully written to include particular sound and spellings.

The Storybooks are graded so your child can progress with confidence from easy words to harder ones. There are four levels - Blue (the easiest), Green, Purple and Turquoise (the hardest). Each level is linked to one of the core *Superphonics Books*.

ISBN 0 340 79575 1

Text copyright © 2002 Gill Munton
Illustrations copyright © 2002 Ian Cunliffe

Editorial by Gill Munton
Design by Sarah Borny

The rights of Gill Munton and Ian Cunliffe to be identified as the author and illustrator of this Work have been asserted by them in accordance with the Copyright, Designs and Patents Act 1988.

First published in Great Britain 2002

10 9 8 7 6 5 4 3 2

First published in 2002 by Hodder Children's Books, a division of Hodder Headline Limited, 338 Euston Road, London NW1 3BH

Printed in China by WKT Company Ltd

A CIP record is registered by and held at the British Library.

Target words

All the Green Storybooks focus on the following sounds:

Double consonants, e.g. **ss** as in **boss** | Blended consonants, e.g. **ng** as in **ring**

Two or three consonants together, e.g. **spr** as in **sprang**, **mp** as in **jump**

These target words are featured in the book

across	grass	will	o'clock
Bagsniff	off	yelled	ping
Hall	rubbish		ring
Bagsniff's	running	banging	sack
bell	skidded	black	sacked
boss	slammed	brushing	shocked
brass	snapped	clicking	sitting
call	Skull	clung	spat
cross	still	frock	sprang
fuss	wall	going	thick
giggling	walls	gong	thing
grabbed	well	hanging	things

trick	damp	jump	pink
swinging	desk	jumped	skin
wings	drifted	just	slugs
wrong	felt	lamp	soft
	gasped	land	Spook
and	grand	landed	swished
bump	help	last	switch
clanking	himself	mist	think
crept	jolt	next	went
daft			

(Words containing sounds and spellings practised in the Blue Storybooks have been used in the story, too.)

Other words

Also included are some common words (e.g. **away**, **very**) which your child will be learning in his or her first few years at school.

A few other words have been used to help the story to flow.

Reading the book

1 Make sure you and your child are sitting in a quiet, comfortable place.

2 Tell him or her a little about the story, without giving too much away:

Spook and Skull are ghosts - but they're not very good ones!

This will give your child a mental picture; having a context for a story makes it easier to read the words.

3 Read the target words (above) together. This will mean that you can both enjoy the story without having to spend too much time working out the words. Help your child to sound out each word (e.g. **d-e-s-k**) before saying the whole word.

4 Let your child read the story aloud. Help him or her with any difficult words and discuss the story as you go along. Stop now and again to ask your child to predict what will happen next. This will help you to see whether he or she has understood what has happened so far.

Above all, enjoy the story, and praise your child's reading!

Ruth Miskin's

Superphonics®

Green Storybook

Spook and Skull

Illustrated by Ian Cunliffe

Hodder Children's Books

a division of Hodder Headline Limited

Skull was sitting at his desk.

"Just one more job," he said.
"Ten o'clock, at Bagsniff Hall."

"OK, boss," said Spook,
as he drifted through the door.

"Now, have we got it all?"
Skull went on.

"The box of bats' wings?"

"Yes, boss!"

"The thing that goes ping?"

"Yes, boss!"

"The sack of slugs?"

"Yes, boss!"

"The bag of things that go bump in the night?"

"Yes, boss!"

"Then off we go!"

It was a black, black night.
Thick mist clung to the mossy walls
of Bagsniff Hall.

Skull sprang from bush to bush,
and Spook crept across
the damp grass.

"Here we are!" said Skull.

"It's very grand!" gasped Spook.

"Rubbish!" snapped Skull.
"Don't make such a fuss!
Now ring the bell,
and then we'll run away."

"I thought Baron Bagsniff
would do the running away,"
said Spook to himself.

When Baron Bagsniff came
to the door, Skull and Spook
rushed away, giggling.

"You go through the wall,"
Skull told Spook,
"and I'll go down the chimney."

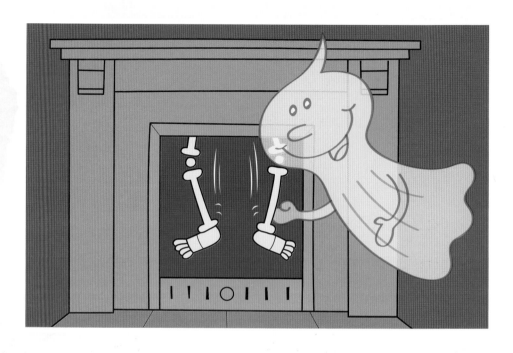

He landed in the hall.

He felt something soft

brushing his leg.

"Help! Help!" he yelled.

"What's wrong?" said Spook.

"It's me, Spook!"

"You foolish phantom!"
yelled Skull.
"You made me jump
out of my skin!"

"You haven't got any skin,"
said Spook to himself.

"Now," said Skull,

"for my first trick!"

He slammed the door.

He gnashed his teeth and spat.

"WHOOO!" he yelled.

"Is he scared yet?" asked Skull.

"No," said Spook.

"Well, then," said Skull,
"for my next trick ... "

He jumped up and grabbed
the lampshade, swinging about
and clicking his legs.

"AAAAAAAAARRGH!" he yelled.

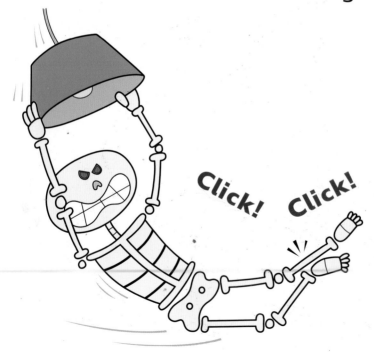

Click! Click!

"Is he scared yet?"

"No," said Spook.

Skull landed on the mat
with a jolt.
"My last trick will -
well, do the trick," he said.

He grabbed a helmet
that was hanging on the wall,
and put it on.

He skidded across the hall,
clanking his helmet
and banging a big brass gong.

"There!" he gasped.
"I bet he's scared now!"

"Um - I think he's still in
the land of nod," said Spook.

Skull looked cross.

"Well, I've done my bit," he said.

"It's up to you now.

Go into Baron Bagsniff's bedroom,

and swish your frock at him!"

"My FROCK?" said Spook
to himself.

"And switch his lamp off first!"
Skull went on.

"Oh, I can't do that!" said Spook,
shocked.

"Why not?"

"Well - I'm not very good in the dark," said Spook, going a bit pink.

"Not very good in the dark? NOT VERY GOOD IN THE DARK?" asked Skull, flashing his teeth. "What kind of daft spook is NOT VERY GOOD IN THE DARK?"

"My kind," said Spook softly.

"Let's just call it a day!" said Skull.

But then:

"Shh! What's that?" yelled Skull.

"Let's get out of here!"

"Back at last!" gasped Spook.
"Baron Bagsniff's not a bad spook,
is he?"

"Not bad at all," said Skull.
"He can come and work for me!
You're sacked!"